BELLE'S CHRISTMAS CAROL

STEPHEN LOMER

stephenlomer.com

ISBN: **1979651760**
ISBN-13: **978-1979651769**

DEDICATION

I dedicate *Belle's Christmas Carol* to the extraordinary David Coffee, who has brought the role of Scrooge to life for so long and delighted so many.

CONTENTS

ACKNOWLEDGMENTS

A huge thank you and tip of the hat to
Charles Dickens, for his masterpiece
*A Christmas Carol in Prose, Being a Ghost-Story of
Christmas,* without which *Belle's Christmas Carol*
would never exist.

PREFACE

Okay, so, about this book.

I just want you to be aware that it is, in essence, a retelling of Charles Dickens' *A Christmas Carol*. Well, not so much a retelling as a recasting, I suppose. It's really hard to explain. You should probably just read it and then we can have an intelligent discussion about it.

Just know that Ebenezer Scrooge, the Cratchit family, Jacob Marley, the ghosts, and all of the other familiar characters are here, doing pretty much what Dickens had them doing, but I went and built it all out and looked at it through a different lens, if that makes sense. Again, it's just easier if you read it and tell me what you think.

Enjoy!

STEPHEN LOMER

CHAPTER ONE

Belle made her way about town, stepping carefully as to avoid spots of drifted snow and patches of ice hiding amongst the cobblestones. Slung over her right arm was a shopping basket of enormous proportions, and it would not do for her to tumble and cause herself injury—to say nothing of the damage she could inflict upon so many carefully collected items—this close to the holiday. Christmas Eve had crept up on her with insidious stealth, and she could still scarcely believe it was already here.

She turned left down a narrow side street and stopped as she came upon a nondescript door nestled in among various homes and shops. A bell jingled merrily as she pushed the door open and let herself in.

3

The room beyond resembled nothing so much as a workshop that was steadily, sinuously overtaking living quarters. Drawings and blueprints, and bits and pieces of things either in the process of being assembled or disassembled, covered every surface.

"Arthur!" called Belle brightly. "It's Belle. Are you at home?"

Up through a nearby pile of metal pieces popped a gentleman's head. He was unkempt; finger-shaped swatches of dirt were smeared across his softly lined face, but his wide smile was genuine and endearing.

"Belle! Welcome!"

"Merry Christmas to you, Arthur."

A look of confusion contorted Arthur's features.

"Christmas already? Wasn't it just July?"

"Dear Arthur. You really must make an effort to get out more."

"Indeed," replied Arthur, carefully standing. "I must."

Belle cast her eyes across the assorted workbenches.

"So! Do you have it?"

Arthur's face became alight.

"Yes! I do! Wait here just a moment!"

4

He disappeared under a nearby table and rummaged for a few moments. When he emerged, he held in his dirty fingers a small bottle of pink liquid.

"It arrived just a few days ago," he said with a winsome smile. "I had to call in many a favor to acquire it."

Belle reached out and took the bottle, examining its contents.

"Does it work?"

"It does! I used it on several mice, a goat, and a horse. And, inadvertently, on myself. Regardless, the effect was instantaneous! It should suit your purposes well."

"Wonderful. And remind me, again, what it is called?"

"Ether."

Belle's next stop was a few streets over—a barber shop doing brisk business as gentlemen made themselves presentable for holiday dinners and parties. She climbed the few steps to the front door and entered.

The quiet chatter of the shop fell dead silent as all of the men within realized that there was suddenly a woman in their midst. They all politely stood, even those in the chairs in mid-shave, and Belle smiled.

One of the barbers stepped forward.

"A very Merry Christmas to you, Belle," said he, with a small bow.

"And to you as well!" she replied. "Is my uncle available?"

The barber inclined his head toward a door in the back, then leaned in and whispered, "Taking a short nap."

"In the middle of the day? On Christmas Eve? Oh, he is *incorrigible!*"

Belle crossed the room and passed straight through a door that opened into a small, cramped storeroom. There, among boxes and crates piles along the walls, lay a man on a small cot, snoring softly.

"Uncle Morgan!" cried Belle.

The old man jerked awake and flailed in disorientation for a few moments. Upon recovering his bearings, and looked blearily up at his niece.

"Angels and saints preserve us, Belle! What are you trying to do, send me off to the choir invisible?"

"It'd do you right!" Belle chided. "Why aren't you tending to your barber shop?"

Morgan rose shakily to his feet and stretched out his back.

"Because I'm a tired old man and there's more than enough barbers to meet the demand."

A beguiling grin cleft Belle's features. "Oh, but no one can make a customer so handsome as you can."

Morgan gave this pronouncement consideration.

"Aye. That's true," replied Morgan, and they both laughed.

"Do you have what I requested?" asked Belle.

"Yes, I do have. Where've they gotten to now ... ?"

He took some time examining a few nearby crates, and then lifted the lid off of one. Packed in straw were very small glass bottles with atomizers attached to them.

"There you are. We use these to spray scented oils into men's beards. I cannot for the life of me imagine what use you could have for them, but if use you have, they are yours to do with as you please."

Belle helped herself to a dozen bottles and stashed them in her basket. She then kissed Morgan on the cheek.

"Thank you, dear uncle. A Merry Christmas to you and Aunt Lily."

"And the same to you, my dear. We'll see you for New Year's?"

"I look forward to it."

Belle was still out and about as the day's shadows began to grow longer. She approached a drab, unwelcoming building on a corner, first slowing and then coming to a full stop underneath a peeling sign that read SCROOGE & MARLEY'S. Through the frosted windows she could see Ebenezer Scrooge, old and craggy and miserable, berating his meek clerk, Bob Cratchit. Scrooge was shouting so loudly that Belle could hear him from the street as clearly as if they were nose to nose.

"If it were up to me," cried Scrooge, "every idiot who goes around with 'Merry Christmas!' on his lips would be boiled in his own pudding and buried with a stake of holly through his heart!"

He fell to grumbling and muttering, and as he did, two portly gentlemen passed Belle on the sidewalk. They both tipped their hats and wished her a Merry Christmas, and then entered Scrooge's counting house, leaving the door open so that Belle is able to hear their exchange.

"Scrooge and Marley's, I believe," the first portly gentleman commenced. "Have I the pleasure of addressing Mr. Scrooge or Mr. Marley?"

"Mr. Marley has been dead these seven years," Scrooge retorted. "He died seven years ago, this very night."

"Ah. Well, we have no doubt his generosity is well represented by his surviving partner. At this festive time of the year, Mr. Scrooge, it is more than usually desirable that we should make some slight provision for the poor and destitute, who suffer greatly at the present time. Many thousands are in want of common necessities. Hundreds of thousands are in want of common comforts, sir."

Scrooge raised his head from his ledger and considered the man.

"Are there no prisons?" asked he.

"Plenty of prisons."

"And the union workhouses? Are they still in operation?"

"They are. Though I wish I could say they were not."

"Oh!" exclaimed Scrooge, with a wretched approximation of a smile. "I was afraid, from what you said at first, that something had occurred to stop them in their useful course. I'm very glad to hear it."

The second portly gentleman stepped forward. "Erhm. A few of us are endeavoring to raise a fund to buy the poor some meat and drink, and means of warmth. We choose this time, because it is a time, of all others, when want is keenly felt, and abundance rejoices. What shall I put you down for?"

"Nothing!"

"Ah! You wish to be anonymous."

"I wish to be left alone!" groused Scrooge. "Since you ask me what I wish, gentlemen, that is my answer. I don't make merry myself at Christmas and I can't afford to make idle people merry. I help to support the establishments I have mentioned. Those who are badly off must go there."

The two portly men exchanged a scandalized look. "Many would rather die!" said the first.

"If they would rather die they had better do it, and decrease the surplus population! Good afternoon, gentlemen!"

The two men gathered their hats and left in stunned disbelief, making sure to give the front door to the counting house a proper slam. As they disappeared into the gathering twilight, Belle leaned forward, watching the counting house carefully, leaving herself prey to Scrooge's nephew Fred, who snuck up upon her.

"Looking awfully suspicious, Belle!"

Belle cried out in surprise, and Scrooge looked up at the sound. Thankfully the glass was too fogged, and Belle and Fred too far away, for Scrooge to make either of them out. Belle swatted at the young man.

"Fred, you scamp! I nearly died of fright!"

"My deepest apologies, Belle. There are times when I simply cannot help myself."

He glanced over at the counting house.

"Have you had the opportunity to sneak in yet?"

"No. There were two gentlemen collecting for the poor, and their girth would have been ideal cover, but Ebenezer showed them the door with too great haste."

"Imagine that. Well fear not, Belle. I shall keep him well distracted for you."

Belle nodded as Fred angled toward Scrooge's door. He looked back at Belle, winked, and threw the door open wide.

"A Merry Christmas, uncle! God save you!"

"Bah! Humbug!" said Scrooge by way of greeting.

"Christmas a humbug, uncle? You don't mean that, I am sure!"

"I do. Merry Christmas! What right have you to be merry? What reason have you to be merry? You're poor enough."

"Come, then! What right have you to be dismal? What reason have you to be morose? You're rich enough."

"Bah! Humbug!"

"Oh, don't be cross, uncle."

From her vantage point, Belle spied Fred rounding to the other side of Scrooge's desk and heard the creak of old wood as Scrooge turned in his chair to face Fred and continue the conversation.

Belle tiptoed in and snuck over to Bob Cratchit's desk, her eyes fixed on Scrooge and Fred, Bob also watching the two men closely.

"What else can I be when I live in such a world of fools as this?" continued Scrooge. "Merry Christmas! Pooh upon Merry Christmas! What's Christmas time to you but a time for paying bills without money? A time for finding yourself a year older, but not an hour richer? A time for balancing your books and never finding balance?"

"Uncle!"

"Nephew! Keep Christmas in your own way, and let me keep it in mine."

Scrooge made to turn his chair back and Belle froze. Fred grabbed one of the chair's armrests to ensure the old man remain turned away from the door.

"Keep it? But you *don't* keep it."

"Let me leave it alone, then. Much good may it do you! Much good it has ever done you!"

Belle arrived at Bob's desk. Bob slowly and carefully handed Belle a key, and she stashed it in her basket. She mouthed the words *See you this evening!* and Bob nodded enthusiastically.

"There are many things from which I might have derived good, by which I have not profited, I dare say," Fred went on. "Christmas among the rest. But I am sure I have always thought of Christmas time, when it has come round, as a good time. A kind, forgiving, charitable, pleasant time. The only time I know of, in the long year, when men and women seem by one consent to open their shut-up hearts freely, and to think of people below them as if they really were fellow passengers to the grave, and not

13

another race of creatures bound on other journeys."

Belle slipped out the front door and moved a few paces down the sidewalk, still listening to the exchange.

"And therefore, uncle, though it has never put a scrap of gold or silver in my pocket, I believe that it has done me good, and will do me good, and I say, God bless it!"

Belle heard Bob applauding this last line, and then the menacing creak of Scrooge's chair as he slowly turned toward him.

"Let me hear another sound from you," said Scrooge lowly but clearly, "and you'll keep your Christmas by losing your situation!"

A pregnant pause followed, then Scrooge turned his chair back to Fred.

"You're quite a powerful speaker, sir. I wonder you don't go into Parliament."

"Don't be angry, uncle. Come! Dine with us tomorrow."

"I'll see you in hell first!"

"But why? Why?"

Scrooge paused for a moment.

"Let me ask you a question, Fred. Why did you get married?"

"Why did I get married?"

"Yes. For what reason?"

"Well—because I fell in love!"

"Because you fell in love! That's the only one thing in the world more ridiculous than Merry Christmas! Good afternoon."

Fred sighed.

"I want nothing from you. I ask nothing of you. Why cannot we be friends?"

"Good afternoon."

"I am sorry, with all my heart, to find you so resolute. We have never had any quarrel to which I have been a party. But I have made the offer to you in the spirit of Christmas, and I'll keep my Christmas humor to the last. So to you, uncle, I say—Merry Christmas!"

"Good afternoon."

"And a happy New Year!"

"Good afternoon!"

As Fred left the counting house to join Belle on the sidewalk, Scrooge continued muttering angrily.

Fred and Belle walked the length of the block and turned a corner before speaking.

"So there you have it. My annual appeal to my uncle to join my family and me for Christmas turkey. At least this year it served a purpose! It did serve a purpose, did it not? You retrieved the key, didn't you?"

Belle smiled and withdrew the key from her basket. Fred smiled as well.

"Excellent. Well then, I shall see you at the theater this evening?"

"Indeed," said Belle. "You have your lines and blocking committed to memory, I trust?"

"Do you jest? This may very well be the most important night in my uncle's life. On my soul I would never risk anything going awry. I am prepared."

"Wonderful! This evening, then!"

Her final stop was the theatre on High Street, where her brother-in-law was in charge of the most complicated and intricate bits of her overarching plan. She had a great deal of faith in Edward, for he had cobbled together magnificent productions with little more than bits of string and balls of fluff, and if anyone could help Belle see her scheme through to the end, it was he.

Belle arrived, somewhat breathless as she was no longer as young as once she was, to see Edward upon the stage, running his actors, stage managers, production men, and prop people through their paces. She reached the orchestra pit and called to him.

"Hello, Edward, and a Merry Christmas to you!"

Edward turned, smiled, leapt over the footlights, and embraced her warmly.

"And a very Merry Christmas to you, Belle!"

"The plans are continuing apace, I see," said Belle, admiring all of the movement and bluster along the length of the stage.

"Indeed. We will be ready for tonight," Edward said, smiling, but Belle could see that his smile did not reach his eyes.

"Edward?" she said softly, so as not to be heard by the company. "Is something troubling you?"

Edward took her gently by the elbow and led her halfway up the aisle, away from curious ears.

"Belle," he said, "you know that I would do anything for my brother, and by extension, anything for you."

"I do."

"But this production ... its cost has been dear. I have sunk every farthing of the company's savings into it. If it fails to produce the desired result ... "

"Oh, but how could it fail?" asked Belle. "With all of this talent, with every man,

17

woman, and child giving all that they have? Oh, Edward. It will be a rousing success, rest assured of that!"

Edward smiled, truly smiled, and both were, for the moment, mollified. "Were you able to secure the sedative?" he asked.

"Yes," said Belle, rummaging in her basket. "Ether. I have two bottles, and several small atomizers that will make administration a simple matter."

"And the key?"

"Yes, I stopped into Scrooge and Marley's just before I came here. I had thought to sneak in whilst two gentlemen collected ... that is, *attempted* to collect for the poor and destitute. But then Ebenezer's nephew Fred arrived and provided intentional distraction. Scrooge took no notice of me, and Mister Cratchit was able to hand me the spare key surreptitiously. We will have no trouble gaining ingress at Scrooge's tonight."

"My goodness, Belle," said Edward. "Have you ever given thought to the life of a spy?"

Dusk had begun to gather as Belle made her way home down the snowy side streets, hailing the festive carolers who stood on nearly every street corner, filling the air with a joyous sound.

She was nearly at her own street when she stopped, thought for a moment, and turned down a different side street. A few doors along, she knocked at the front door of number 9 and waited.

The door swung open, and standing there was the dark-haired figure of Charles Dickens, a well-known if not terribly successful author. Charles' face lit up when he saw her.

"Belle!" he exclaimed. "Come in, please, come in!"

She crossed the threshold and he guided her to a chair by the front window that looked out onto the street. A merry fire crackled in the hearth, and the room glowed with holiday warmth. He sat down across from her, smiling broadly.

"Can I get you something? A spirit to fight the evening cold, perhaps?"

"Oh that I would, but I cannot stay," said Belle. "There is so much yet to do in preparation for tonight. I only wanted to convey my gratitude to you. For writing such a wonderful and heartwarming script for tonight's production."

"It was my pleasure. I only hope that it is successful in changing Mister Scrooge's nature. I have seen first-hand the misery and plight of the poor and destitute. I know the struggles of the common man, to put roof over head and food on the table. Mister Scrooge's wealth could do much to ease the burdens of our friends and neighbors."

"I cannot imagine a soul on this earth who could hear your words and not be changed evermore."

"I will cling to that hope with all the strength I am able," Dickens said. "Belle? Would it be all right if I joined you and the others tonight?"

"Of course it would. But why?"

"I do not think I will be able to stand the suspense of not knowing how the evening turns out!" Dickens laughed.

"I understand perfectly. I do not think I would be able to stand the suspense either. By all means, come along tonight. Meet me at the theatre in two hours' time."

"I will. And as likely as not, giddy as a schoolboy."

Belle arrived home a short while later. As the door swung open, she found herself mobbed by her younger children, all crying out with gladness to see her and throwing their small arms about her person.

"Oh, my dear children!" said Belle, removing her traveling cloak with some effort. "How I have missed you in the short while I have been gone! Are you all ready for Christmas?"

After assuring her that they were, indeed, ready, she kissed them all in turn and chivvied them off to the parlor.

"Belle?" came her husband's deep voice from the drawing room. "A word?"

She entered the room, closing the door behind her. The figure of her husband was framed in shadow by the window that overlooked the back garden. Snow had begun gently falling.

"How do tonight's plans progress?"

"As far as I can tell, everything is ready."

"And you still believe that you will be able to transform Mister Scrooge?"

"I do."

"And you maintain that your desire in changing Mister Scrooge is purely altruistic?"

"What else would it be?"

Edgar stepped toward her and the candlelight caught his face. He seemed deeply troubled.

"I understand that if Mister Scrooge can be made to see the error of his ways, that the poor and wretched will benefit greatly from his generosity. But is that your sole motivation?"

"Edgar, the hour grows late. Please speak plainly, I beg you."

Edgar stepped even closer. "Belle ... do you still love him?"

"Oh, Edgar," Belle said with a small smile and a gentle hand on his cheek. "No. True, I loved him once, but a very long time ago. He is no longer the man to whom I gave my heart."

"But tonight you work to restore that man."

Belle shook her head. "That man is long gone, long gone. Tonight I work to create a new man, one whose generosity knows no bounds and whose heart bursts with the joy of Christmas."

Edgar still looked uneasy.

"My dearest, I loved my parents. I love my brother and sister. I love our children. And I love you. That is all you need know."

Edgar grinned as he nodded. "Then I will delay you no longer. Mary waits for you in her room. She is the very mirror image of you at that age."

"Excellent," Belle said. "Then she and I must be off."

STEPHEN LOMER

CHAPTER TWO

Night crept over the city with stealth, and brought with it a bitter frost. Belle, Edward, and the entire theatre company waited in the theatre's lobby as they watched and waited for the signal that Scrooge was approaching his residence.

A few blocks away, a young newsboy stood in the cold and dark outside a melancholy tavern. He watched as Scrooge ate a cheap dinner and thumbed through a pile of newspapers on the table.

Eventually Scrooge rose, threw his cloak around his shoulders, and moved toward the tavern's front door. The boy took off running down several streets, weaving in and out of shoppers and carolers as he made his way to the theater. The newsboy skidded into view and waved, and Belle turned to Edward.

"It is time," she said. Edward nodded to a stagehand dressed head-to-toe in black and carrying a curious lantern lined with mirrors and displaying a complex cutout of a man's face on one side. The stagehand braved the bitter night air, and Belle, dressed in her warmest attire, followed to observe.

The stagehand ran ahead and secreted himself in the shadows to one side of the stairs leading up to Scrooge's residence. The old man arrived presently, and as he fumbled with his keys for the lock, the stagehand lit the odd lantern. The light within shone through the cutout face, and displayed upon Scrooge's door knocker the glowing, otherworldly face of his deceased partner, Jacob Marley.

By great good fortune or divine providence, Scrooge was so shocked and terrified at the image of Marley's spectral face that he paid no mind to the stagehand nor the lantern projecting it. And by an even greater stroke of luck, Scrooge hid his eyes behind his sleeve for just a moment, allowing the stagehand to extinguish the lantern seamlessly.

When the candle was blown out and Marley had disappeared, the stagehand slipped back into the shadows, again unnoticed by Scrooge.

The old man examined the knocker closely, and, deciding that it was simply a knocker, said "Pooh! Pooh!" and closed the door with a bang.

The stagehand leaned out and watched closely through the windows as Scrooge made his way up the grand staircase to his chambers, then made haste back to the theater.

"He has retired to his chambers!" the stagehand told Belle and Edward upon his return, and there was a great deal of excited murmuring among the company.

"The time is upon us!" Edward called out to those gathered. "Let us be off!" And off they went.

And what a strange sight would have met curious eyes if the streets were not so deserted as Christmas drew near! Throngs of actors and actresses dressed in the most unusual fashions; more stagehands dressed entirely in black carrying boxes and baskets and sacks filled with a vast assortment of items, along with ropes, ladders, and hooks; and gripped in nearly everyone's hand, even the smallest hands, great swaths of black cloth.

The parade made its way to Scrooge's residence and Belle used her key as quietly and quickly as was possible. After a cursory look around the cold, dark, high-ceilinged entrance, she gestured at the large group awaiting ingress and they all moved inside.

You would think that so many figures making their way across the creaky old boards of Scrooge's first floor would make a terrible racket, but in this case you would be wrong, for these were men and women of the theater, much accustomed to making their way around backstage without rousing the audience. Even those who were not members of the troupe, for in truth the entire Cratchit family and Scrooge's nephew Fred and his wife and friends were all among the intruders, had been well-trained by Edward in the art of stealth in their rehearsals for tonight's performance, so they were no louder or more obtrusive than church-mice.

Belle led them through a pair of double doors to the left of the main staircase and into a cavernous ballroom, long disused and forgotten. After a few moments' observation, the crew set to their tasks.

And oh, what a well-oiled machine they were! Like monkeys on vines they climbed to the rafters and hung the black cloths from ropes across the ceiling, blotting out the light streaming in through the windows. It cast the ballroom into utter and all-consuming darkness but provided them a well-lit area—a backstage, for want of a better term—to allow them to coordinate the production. Furniture rolled thither and yon, painted canvases were unrolled and attached to wooden frames, and costumes and makeup were tended to. After a short while, and a final once-over by Edward and Belle, the cast and crew were prepared.

Belle stood behind a black curtain near the door, watching as the actor who would be portraying Jacob Marley had long lengths of chain cuffed to his wrists as his costume and ghostly makeup glowed with the phosphorus from the apothecary, and began to fret. She grabbed Edward by the elbow and pulled him aside.

"I'm afraid," said Belle.

"Of what?"

"There is so much involved. So very much that can go wrong."

"Belle," said Edward soothingly. "We have rehearsed and rehearsed. Everyone here is a professional. Have faith. And anyway," he said, grinning, "it is much too late to turn back now."

Belle nodded. The makeup master stage-whispered that Marley was ready, and as Belle looked upon him, she could not agree more. He looked so much like Marley, but in truth a seven-years-dead Marley, that she could not suppress a shudder.

"Go!" stage-whispered Edward in reply, and Marley dragged his chains, along with the steel cash-boxes, keys, padlocks, ledgers, deeds, and heavy purses wrought in them, noisily out into the entranceway.

CHAPTER THREE

Belle and Edward stood at the foot of the grand staircase, watching and listening as the actor playing Marley's ghost climbed the stairs and forced his way into Scrooge's chambers, moaning and howling in agony.

"When he engages Scrooge, his skills as a great improviser will be revealed," whispered Edward to Belle.

"How now!" they heard Scrooge cry, caustic and cold as ever. "What do you want with me?"

"Much!" replied Marley.

"Who are you?"

"Ask me who I was."

"Who were you then?" said Scrooge, raising his voice. "You're particular, for a phantom."

31

"In life I was your partner, Jacob Marley."

"Can you—can you sit down?" asked Scrooge.

Belle looked at Edward in alarm. Could the actor sit down? They had never tried, for this was a most unexpected question from Scrooge.

"I can," they heard Marley say without hesitation.

"Do it, then."

Belle listened closely and heard a further rattle of chains as Marley must have taken a seat. She breathed a small sigh of relief. It was then that she noticed that in addition to Edward, she was joined at the foot of the staircase by Charles Dickens, who appeared to be listening intently to the conversation upstairs.

"You don't believe in me," said Marley.

"I don't," said Scrooge.

"What evidence would you have of my reality beyond that of your senses?"

"I don't know," said Scrooge.

"Why do you doubt your senses?"

"Because," said Scrooge, "a little thing affects them. A slight stomach disorder can alter them. You may be an undigested bit of beef, a blot of mustard, a crumb of cheese, a fragment of an underdone potato. There's more of gravy than of grave about you, whatever you are!"

There was a pause, and Belle's pulse quickened. Had something gone wrong? But then Scrooge continued.

"Do you see this toothpick?" said Scrooge.

"I do," replied Marley.

"You are not looking at it," said Scrooge.

"But I see it," said Marley, "notwithstanding."

Belle smiled at this bit of flourish.

"Well," returned Scrooge, "if I swallowed this, I would find myself persecuted by a legion of goblins for the rest of my day, all of my mind's own creation. Humbug, I tell you! Humbug!"

At this, Marley raised a frightful cry, and shook his chains with such a dismal and appalling noise that Belle thought for a fleeting moment that an apparition really had entered Scrooge's chambers. She heard the sound of Scrooge falling to his knees.

"Mercy!" he said. "Dreadful apparition, why do you trouble me?"

"Man of the earth!" replied Marley. "Do you believe in me or not?"

"I do," said Scrooge. "I must. But why do spirits walk the earth, and why do they come to me?"

"It is required of every man," Marley returned, "that the spirit within him should walk alongside his fellow man, and travel far and wide. And if that spirit does not do so in life, it is condemned to do so after death. It is doomed to wander through the world—oh, woe is me!—and witness what it cannot share, but might have shared on earth!"

Again Marley raised a cry, and shook his chains. Edward, listening intently, smiled and nodded his approval of the performance.

"You are chained," said Scrooge, trembling. "Tell me why."

"I wear the chain I forged in life," replied Marley. "I made it link by link, and yard by yard. I made it of my own free will, and I wore it of my own free will. Would you like to know the weight and length of the strong coil you bear yourself? It was as full and as heavy and as long as this, seven Christmas Eves ago. You have worked on it since. It is a thick and lengthy chain!"

"Jacob," Scrooge said, imploringly. "Old Jacob Marley, tell me more. Speak comfort to me, Jacob!"

Belle and Edward exchanged a meaningful glance. Scrooge sounded as though he seemed truly convinced by their apparition.

"I have none to give," Marley replied. "It comes from somewhere else, Ebenezer Scrooge, and is conveyed by others to other men. Nor can I tell you what I would like to tell you. I am permitted very little more. I cannot rest, I cannot stay, I cannot linger anywhere. My spirit never walked beyond our counting-house—mark me!—in life my spirit never roamed beyond the narrow limits of our money-changing hole, and weary journeys lie before me!"

"You must have been very slow about it, Jacob," Scrooge observed, in a businesslike manner.

"Slow?" Marley repeated.

"Seven years dead," mused Scrooge. "And traveling all the time?"

"The whole time," said Marley. "No rest, no peace. The never-ending torture of remorse."

"You travel fast?" said Scrooge.

"On the wings of the wind," replied Marley.

"You might have gotten over quite a bit of ground in seven years," said Scrooge.

Marley, upon hearing this, cried out again, and clanked his chains so hideously in the dead silence of the night, that Belle feared a constable might come running and arrest him as a nuisance.

"Oh! Captive, bound, and chained," cried Marley, "knowing that no amount of regret can make amends for my misused opportunities in life! That was me! Oh! That was me!"

"But you were always a good man of business, Jacob," faltered Scrooge.

"Business!" cried the Ghost. "Mankind was my business. The common welfare was my business! Charity, mercy, kindness, and benevolence were all my business! My dealings were only a drop of water in the vast ocean of my business!"

Belle risked a whisper to Edward, nodding toward Charles, who was thoroughly absorbed in the dialogue above: "My favorite part. Mister Dickens' most profound words to be spoken."

"At this time of the year," Marley said, "I suffer most. Why did I walk through crowds of fellow beings with my eyes down, and never look up to that blessed star that led the wise men to a poor abode? Were there no

36

poor homes to which its light would have taken me?"

At this moment, Marley gave a great, dramatic pause. It seemed Scrooge might be holding his breath, for surely Belle, Edward, and Charles were.

"Hear me!" he cried at last. "My time is nearly gone."

"I will," said Scrooge. "But don't be hard upon me! Don't be harsh, Jacob! I beg you!"

"I am not allowed to tell you how it is that I appear before you in a shape that you can see. I have sat invisible beside you so many days now. That is part of my penance. I am here tonight to warn you, that you have a chance and hope of escaping my fate. A chance and hope that I have procured for you, Ebenezer."

"You were always a good friend to me," said Scrooge. "Thank you!"

"You will be haunted," resumed Marley, "by three spirits."

At this cue, Edward disappeared from Belle's side, but Charles remained, still fully attentive to the scene playing out above them.

"Is that the chance and hope you mentioned, Jacob?" Scrooge demanded, in a faltering voice.

"It is."

"I—I think I'd rather not," said Scrooge.

"Without their visits," said Marley, "you cannot hope to escape the path I tread. Expect the first tomorrow, when the bell tolls one."

Edward returned, with four black-clad stagehands in tow, and resumed listening.

"Couldn't I take them all at once and be done with it, Jacob?" hinted Scrooge.

"Expect the second on the next night at the same hour. The third upon the next night when the last stroke of twelve has ceased ringing. You will not see me again, but for your own sake, remember what has passed between us!"

Belle knew that this was the end of the scripted monologue. She could picture in her mind's eye the Marley actor reaching a white, glowing hand toward Scrooge, and with the old man likely cowering in his chair, eyes closed tight shut, squeezing a cloud of ether in the Scrooge's face from the atomizer slid up his ghostly sleeve.

A soft thud, and then silence.

CHAPTER FOUR

"Now!" called Marley from the top of the stairs, and the four stagehands flew up the staircase. They reappeared in short order, each of them holding a bony limb of the unconscious Scrooge. While they carried him with care down the stairs, still more stagehands dragged a bed much like Scrooge's from a downstairs bedchamber and into the darkened ballroom. Upon this bed they laid Scrooge and tucked him under the bedclothes.

Everyone vanished to their stations as Scrooge began to stir. In the furthest corner a large bell had been set, and Edward himself lifted the hammer and began to strike it. Within the vast echoing room, it was indistinguishable from the church bell. Scrooge woke to the sound.

"Twelve!" he said into the pitch blackness. "Why, it isn't possible that I have slept through a whole day and far into another night. It isn't possible that anything has happened to the sun, and this is twelve noon!"

He sat up, listening intently. There was no noise of people running to and fro, and making a great stir, as there unquestionably would have been if night had become bright day.

Then Edward struck the bell again.

Gong.

"A quarter past," said Scrooge.

Gong.

"Half past!" said Scrooge.

Gong.

"A quarter to it," said Scrooge.

Gong.

"The hour itself," said Scrooge, triumphantly, "and nothing else!"

He spoke before the hour bell had finished sounding, which it did with a deep, dull, hollow, melancholy tone.

Behind the curtains, Belle nodded toward Catherine, a beautiful young creature who had been the central figure in many a production. Though still beautiful, she was barely recognizable, her face covered with white powder laced with the same phosphorous that had made Jacob Marley glow, and a tall wig adorned with holly and a crown with carefully placed candles. She stood upon a small platform seated on rolling casters, and two stagehands hid beneath her diaphanous, voluminous white dress, so that when she moved, she appeared to be floating from place to place. She held in one hand a giant votive, which lit her in a most ghostly fashion.

Catherine approached Scrooge's bed and drew aside the curtains. Scrooge, sitting up from his pillows, found himself face-to-face with the unearthly visitor who drew them.

"Are you the spirit whose coming was foretold to me?" asked Scrooge.

"I am."

The voice was soft and gentle. Low, as if instead of being so close beside him, it were at a great distance.

"Who, and what are you?" Scrooge demanded.

"I am the Ghost of Christmas Past."

"Long past?" inquired Scrooge.

"No. Your past."

Scrooge then inquired what business brought the ghost there.

"Your welfare," said the ghost.

41

Scrooge said he was much obliged, but stated that a night of unbroken rest would have been more conducive to his welfare.

"Your reclamation, then," the Spirit said immediately. "Take heed!"

She put out her hand as she spoke, and clasped him gently by the arm.

"Rise, and walk with me."

Scrooge did as he was asked, and the Ghost guided him in the pitch blackness of the ballroom toward the first tableau that had been prepared. To disguise the sound of the wheels under her gown rolling, sound experts behind the curtains shook large pieces of metal, making a terrible sound that caused Scrooge to jump and huddle closer to his guide.

When the pair had reached their designated location, near the northeast corner of the ballroom, a great oil-lamp spotlight suspended from the ceiling blazed to life. It illuminated a young actor, dressed and made up to appear as a very young Scrooge, sitting alone at a small desk. False walls had been constructed on two sides of him, so to Scrooge's eyes, it appeared that he and the Ghost were staring right through the solid

42

brick and mortar and into the actual schoolroom itself.

"Why, it's me!" exclaimed Scrooge. "Can he see me as I see him?"

"These are just shadows of things that have been," said the Ghost. "They have no consciousness of us."

Scrooge and the Spirit gazed upon the solitary child, reading by his lonesome, apparently neglected by his friends.

"Your lip is trembling," said the Ghost. "And what is that upon your cheek?"

Scrooge muttered, with an unusual hitch in his voice, that it was a pimple. Then, with uncharacteristic speed, he said, in pity for his former self, "Poor boy!" and cried again.

After a time, Scrooge dried his eyes with his cuff. "I wish," he muttered, but then shook his head. "Ah, but it's too late now."

"What is the matter?" asked the Spirit.

"Nothing," said Scrooge. "Nothing. There was a boy singing a Christmas Carol at my door last night. I would like to have given him something. That's all."

The Ghost smiled thoughtfully and waved her hand, saying as she did so, "Let us see another Christmas!"

The spotlight above them darkened, allowing the young man dressed as Scrooge to make a hasty exit as a slightly older boy, also dressed as Scrooge, took his place. When the light blazed once again, the transition appeared seamless.

This young Scrooge was not reading, but walking up and down the false room, agitated. Scrooge looked at the Ghost, and with a mournful shaking of his head, glanced anxiously into the darkness beyond the circle of light that lit the scene.

Out of that darkness scampered a young actress dressed and made up to resemble the boy's younger sister. She ran to him, put her arms around his neck, kissed him, and addressed him as "Dear, dear brother."

"I have come to bring you home, dear brother!" said the child, clapping her tiny hands, and bending down to laugh. "To bring you home, home, home!"

"Home, little Fan?" returned the boy.

"Yes!" said the child gleefully. "Home, for now. Home, forever and ever. Father is so much kinder than he used to be. Home is like heaven! He spoke so gently to me one night when I was going to bed, that I was not afraid to ask him again if you might come home.

44

And he said yes! Yes, you should! He sent me in a coach to bring you! You are never to return here again. But first, we're to be together all Christmas long, and have the merriest time in all the world."

"You are quite a woman, little Fan!" exclaimed the boy.

She clapped her hands and laughed, and stood on tiptoe to embrace him again. Then she began to drag him, in her childish eagerness, toward the darkness, and he accompanied her.

"Always a delicate creature. A strong gust of wind would have carried her away," said the Ghost. "But she had a large heart."

"So she had," cried Scrooge. "You're right, Spirit. A very large heart indeed."

"She died a woman," said the Ghost, "and had, I believe, children."

Backstage, Edward and Belle exchange a horrified look.

"Children?" Edward whispered urgently. He hastened to examine script pages stacked on a nearby plinth. "It's one child, is it not?"

"Yes! One child!" Belle whispers back.

"One child," Scrooge returned.

Catherine realized her mistake and recovered quickly.

45

"True," said the Ghost. "Your nephew."

Scrooge seemed uneasy, and answered curtly, "Yes."

"Come," said the Ghost, and she took Scrooge's hand. The spotlight extinguished and plunged them again into darkness and the terrible noise roared once more as the Ghost was rolled to the next setup, pulling Scrooge along with her.

CHAPTER FIVE

Belle watched anxiously from behind the curtain. The next sequence was a complex and complicated one. A multitude of things could go wrong, and there were many performers with makeup, wigs, and costumes.

"They are the most professional troupe with whom I have ever worked," whispered Edward at her elbow, seeing the unease on her face. "Fear not."

The Ghost moved Scrooge into position, and yet another spotlight blazed into life. This one lit what appeared to be the inside of a factory, and the Ghost asked Scrooge if he knew it.

"Know it?" said Scrooge. "I was apprenticed here!"

An older, portly actor was dressed as an old gentleman in a Welsh wig, sitting behind a high desk. Scrooge cried out in great excitement.

"Why, it's old Fezziwig! Bless his heart. It's Fezziwig, alive again!"

At this, Belle let loose a breath she had been unaware of holding and a huge smile crossed her face. She grabbed Edward's shoulders and shook him in excitement.

"He believes! He truly believes!"

Edward smiled as well.

"Mayhap we benefit from his advanced years and poor eyesight."

"Or his mind is addled with this ether concoction. Oh dear. I should have asked Arthur if it has any lasting effects."

"If it does, let us be grateful that we used it on him and not ourselves."

Old Fezziwig laid down his pen, pulled out his pocket watch, examined it, and replaced it. He rubbed his hands, adjusted his massive waistcoat, laughed heartily, and then called out in a comfortable, oily, rich, fat, jovial voice:

"Ho, there! Ebenezer! Dick!"

Two teenaged actors, one dressed and made up as a teenaged Scrooge, appeared from the darkness. Scrooge recognized the second young man.

"Dick Wilkins!" said Scrooge to the Ghost. "Bless me, yes. There he is! He was very fond of me, Dick was. Poor Dick! Oh dear, oh dear!"

"Ho, my boys!" said Fezziwig. "No more work tonight. It's Christmas Eve, Dick! It's Christmas Eve, Ebenezer! Close up the shutters," cried old Fezziwig, with a sharp clap of his hands, "quicker than a cat can wink its eye!"

The two young men disappeared once again into the darkness, and now the sound effects men imitated the sound of shutters being closed. After twelve of them, the two young men reappeared, panting like racehorses.

"Right!" cried old Fezziwig, skipping down from the high desk with impressive agility. "Clear away, my lads, and let's have lots of room here! Quickly, Dick! Quick, Ebenezer!"

Dick and Ebenezer cleared off boxes that had been set there for that purpose, and produced brooms to sweep the floor. In a trice, the staged warehouse appeared snug and warm and dry.

49

In came a fiddler with a music book. He climbed up the lofty desk and tuned his instrument in preparation to play it. In came a rotund actress of the company portraying Mrs. Fezziwig, wearing an ear-to-ear smile. In came a whole host of actors and actresses, portraying the Fezziwig family; all the young men and women employed in the business; a housemaid, a baker, a cook, and a milkman. A veritable parade of performers pouring out from behind the curtain, into the darkness of the ballroom, and then again into the light for Scrooge to look upon.

The fiddler began to scratch out a tune, and how they all danced! All on their own, then as couples, then in circles around one another, all led in time by the fiddler and in great good spirits by the Fezziwigs, who were still dancing when younger and sprier souls took their leave of the dance floor.

The same bell behind the curtain that had been rung to announce the arrival of the Ghost struck eleven, though more quietly this time, and the ball broke up. Mr. and Mrs. Fezziwig took their stations on the edge of the pool of light, shaking hands with every person individually as he or she vanished into the dark, wishing him or her a Merry Christmas.

During this whole time, Scrooge enjoyed all that he saw, fully immersed in the revelry. It was not until now, when the actors had all disappeared and the spotlight faded, that he remembered the Ghost, and became conscious that she was looking at him, while the light upon her head burnt very clear.

"Oh, Fezziwig," Scrooge said. "One of the finest men who ever lived. And the finest master."

"A small matter," said the Ghost, "to make these silly folks so full of gratitude."

"Small!" echoed Scrooge.

"Isn't it? He has spent but a few pounds of your mortal money: three or four perhaps. Is that so much that he deserves praise?"

"It isn't that," said Scrooge. "It isn't that, Spirit. He had the power to make us happy, to make our service a pleasure. The happiness he gave was as great as if it cost a fortune."

He felt the Spirit's stare and stopped.

"What is the matter?" asked the Ghost.

"Nothing particular," said Scrooge.

"Are you certain?" the Ghost insisted.

"It's," said Scrooge, "It's just that I would like to be able to say a word or two to my clerk right now. That's all."

Behind the curtain, Belle looked over at Bob Cratchit, who had heard every word and whose expression was one of intrigue in the backstage shadows.

The spotlight extinguished and the actress portraying the Ghost had forgotten to grab hold of Scrooge's arm. She groped in the darkness, nearly tumbling off of her moving stage, until her hand at last found his.

"My time grows short," said the Spirit, recovering herself. "Quick!"

They moved to another spot in the ballroom. This had been staged to appear as a small, snow-covered kissing bridge at night, and when the spotlight lit it, you could not tell it apart from the genuine article. The actor who had most recently played Scrooge had engaged in a rapid costume change and deepening of the lines in his makeup and appeared once again as a slightly older Scrooge.

He was not alone, but stood by a fair young girl with tears in her eyes, which sparkled in the light that shone out of the Ghost of Christmas Past. The girl was Belle's

daughter Mary, who truly was the living image
of young Belle.

"Why do you weep?" younger Scrooge
asked.

"It doesn't matter," Mary said, softly. "To
you, it doesn't matter. Another idol has
replaced me. If it can cheer and comfort you
in the future, as I would have tried to do, so
be it."

"What idol has replaced you?" he asked.

"A golden one."

"This is the way of the world!" he said.
"There is nothing so hard as poverty, and
there is nothing so frowned upon as the
pursuit of wealth!"

"You fear the world too much," she
answered, gently. "All your hopes have
merged into one: accumulating wealth until
wealth is all you have. I have seen your nobler
aspirations fall off one by one, until all you
can see is gain. Have I not?"

"So?" he retorted. "I am not changed
toward you."

She shook her head.

"Am I?"

"Our contract is an old one. It was made
when we were both poor and content to be
so, until, eventually, we could improve our lot

in life by our hard work. You are changed. When it was made, you were another man."

"I was a boy," he said impatiently.

"Your heart tells you that you are not what you were," she returned. "I am. When we were one in heart, life held promise. Now that we are two, it holds only misery. I will not say how often or how much I have thought of this. It is enough that I have thought of it. I release you."

"Have I ever asked for release?"

"In words. No. Never."

"In what, then?"

"In a changed nature. In an altered spirit. In everything that made my love worthwhile or valuable to you. If this had never been between us," said the girl, looking mildly, but with steadiness, upon him, "tell me, would you seek me out and try to win me now? No. You would not."

He said with a struggle, "You don't think so."

"Heaven knows I would gladly think otherwise if I could," she answered. "When I have learned a truth like this, I know how strong and irresistible it must be. If you were free today, tomorrow, yesterday, I cannot believe that you would choose a dowerless girl—you, who weigh everything by gain. If you chose her, I know that regret would surely follow. I do. So I release you. With a full heart, for the love of the man you once were."

He was about to speak, but with her head turned from him, she resumed.

"This may cause you pain. Part of me hopes that it does. But the pain will last a very, very brief time, and you will dismiss the memory of it, gladly, as an unprofitable dream, from which you were happy to wake. May you be happy in the life you have chosen!"

She left, and the scene went dim.

Mary scampered back behind the curtain to seek out her mother, but Belle was beside herself with grief.

"Mother!" Mary whispered. "What is it?"

"Oh, pay me no mind, child," Belle said, composing herself, wiping her tears with a handkerchief. "I had heard those words many a time in rehearsal and not had a second thought about them, but seeing that moment with Ebenezer brought back so vividly just now! It caught me unawares. You did wonderfully tonight, Mary. I am so very proud of you."

They embraced, and Mary moved off while Belle returned to the curtain's edge.

"Spirit!" said Scrooge in a broken voice, "remove me from this place."

"I told you these were shadows of the things that have been," said the Ghost. "Do not blame me for what they are!"

"Remove me!" Scrooge exclaimed, "I cannot bear it! Leave me! Take me back. Haunt me no longer!"

The Ghost moved Scrooge back through the darkness toward the bed, and just before arriving at it, squeezed a small bulb hidden in her sleeve. A cloud of ether again enveloped Scrooge's face and his gait became unsteady, his eyes losing all focus.

The stagehands guiding the Ghost slipped out from under her many folds and grabbed Scrooge on either side just as he tipped forward into unconsciousness. Thankfully Scrooge was a very light, very thin man, and they were able to easily hoist him to the mattress and tuck him under his bedclothes as he began to snore softly.

"Reset!" cried Edward from behind the curtain as he saw Scrooge fast asleep, and a flurry of activity filled the ballroom once again. Sets were removed and replaced afresh.

Performers scurried to remove makeup and switch to more contemporary clothes. In all, a great deal of noise and fuss and chaos, and through it all, Scrooge slept like the dead.

STEPHEN LOMER

CHAPTER SIX

Awaking in the middle of a terribly loud snore, and sitting up in bed to get his thoughts together, Scrooge once again found himself surrounded by the impenetrable blackness, and once again heard the production company's bell strike the hour. The toll had barely finished ringing when a spotlight illuminated a figure near the foot of Scrooge's bed.

For the part, Edward had chosen the tallest and broadest member of the troupe, a man called Iain, whose prodigious red beard and wild tangle of long red hair, along with a deep, booming, baritone voice, made him truly something to behold.

Heaped up on the floor around him, to form a kind of throne, were turkeys, geese, game, poultry, great slabs of meat, suckling pigs, long wreaths of sausages, mince pies, plum puddings, barrels of oysters, red-hot chestnuts, cherry-cheeked apples, juicy oranges, luscious pears, cakes, and full bowls of punch, all of which Edward's elite crew had assembled in extraordinary time and with exceptional precision. Iain, in his guise as the next Ghost, sat upon this pile of food, bearing a glowing torch, shaped like a horn of plenty. He held it up high as Scrooge timidly crossed the floor toward him.

"Come!" exclaimed the Ghost. "Come and know me better, man!"

Scrooge hung his head before this Spirit. Belle could see from her vantage that already he did not appear to be the miserable Scrooge he had been.

"I am the Ghost of Christmas Present," said the Spirit. "Look upon me!"

Scrooge did so. He was clothed in a green robe bordered with white fur. This garment hung so loosely on the figure that his barrel chest was laid bare. His feet, observable beneath the ample folds of the garment, were also bare. On his head he wore a holly wreath, set here and there with shining icicles. At his hip was an antique scabbard, but no sword was in it, and the ancient sheath was eaten up with rust. In all, a tremendous achievement by the costuming contingent of Edward's company.

"You have never seen the like of me before!" exclaimed the Spirit.

"Never," said Scrooge.

"Have you never walked alongside the members of my family? My younger brothers, as it were?" pursued the Ghost.

"I don't think I have," said Scrooge. "Have you had many brothers, Spirit?"

"More than eighteen hundred," said the Ghost.

"A tremendous family to provide for," muttered Scrooge.

No one had expected any humor from Scrooge, and Belle watched as the corners of Iain's mouth twitched at this actually quite funny line. But Iain decided to incorporate it on the spot and let forth with a loud, raucous belly laugh, which thankfully, fit his character perfectly.

The Ghost of Christmas Present rose.

"Spirit," said Scrooge submissively, "take me where you will. I was forced to journey last night, but I learned a lesson that is working even now. Tonight, if you have something to teach me, then teach me."

"Touch my robe."

Scrooge did as he was told, and held it tight.

They stepped into the darkness and walked for a moment or two before yet another spotlight blazed. This one seemed to light the interior of a small, shabby home, though in truth, it was more of the theatre company's expertly crafted scenery that made it appear so.

As they watched, the members of the Cratchit family came into view. These were, again, not actors but the real Cratchit family, whose presence had been requested by Belle herself and who had gladly given up their regular Christmas Eve revelry in order to have some small part in the changing of Mr. Scrooge's nature, if it were to be changed.

Up rose Mrs. Cratchit, Bob Cratchit's wife, dressed in a cheap gown made pretty with inexpensive ribbons. She laid the tablecloth, assisted by Belinda Cratchit, second of her daughters, also wearing ribbons, while Master Peter Cratchit plunged a fork into a saucepan of potatoes. And now two smaller Cratchits, boy and girl, came tearing in from the darkness and danced around the table.

"Where is your father then?" said Mrs. Cratchit. "And your brother, Tiny Tim! And Martha wasn't this late last Christmas Day."

"Here's Martha, Mother!" said a girl, appearing as she spoke.

"Here's Martha, Mother!" cried the two young Cratchits. "Hurrah!"

"Why, bless your heart, my dear, how late you are!" said Mrs. Cratchit, kissing Martha a dozen times, and taking off her shawl and bonnet for her.

"We had a great deal of work to finish up last night," replied the girl, "and had to clear away this morning, Mother!"

"Well! Never mind, as long as you're here," said Mrs. Cratchit. "Have a seat at the table, my dear, bless you!"

"No, no! Father's coming," cried the two young Cratchits, who were everywhere at once. "Hide, Martha, hide!"

So Martha hid herself. In came little Bob, the father, with a threadbare coat covering his threadbare clothes, and Tiny Tim on his shoulder. Poor Tiny Tim, he carried a little crutch, and his limbs were supported by an iron frame.

It bears noting that the Cratchits had no son Tim, lame or otherwise. Tim was an invention of Mr. Dickens for the production, as a method of pulling on old Scrooge's heartstrings, and Tim was in reality Owen, the youngest and smallest member of Edward's troupe, though quite talented and naturally gifted on the stage.

"Where's our Martha?" cried Bob Cratchit, looking around.

"Not coming," said Mrs. Cratchit.

"Not coming!" said Bob, his shoulders sagging. "Not coming on Christmas Day?"

Martha came out from behind a closet door, both surprising and delighting him, and ran into his arms, while the two young Cratchits held Tiny Tim and took him off into the shadows.

"And how did little Tim behave?" asked Mrs. Cratchit, when Bob had hugged his daughter to his heart's content.

"As good as gold," said Bob, "Somehow he gets thoughtful, sitting by himself so much, and thinks the funniest things you ever heard. He told me, coming home, that he hoped the people saw him in the church, because he was a cripple, and it might be pleasant for them to remember upon Christmas Day who it was that made lame beggars walk and blind men see."

Bob's voice shook when he told them this, and trembled more when he said that Tiny Tim was growing strong and hearty.

Back came Tiny Tim, leaning on his crutch and escorted by his brother and sister to his little stool on the edge of the circle of light, while Bob, turning up his shabby cuffs, stirred up a drink. Master Peter and the two young Cratchits went to fetch the goose, which they brought in with a great deal of bluster.

Mrs. Cratchit made the gravy; Master Peter mashed the potatoes with vigor; Miss Belinda sweetened up the applesauce; Martha dusted the hot plates; Bob took Tiny Tim beside him at the table; the two young Cratchits set chairs for everybody, not forgetting themselves.

At last the dishes were set, and grace was said. Then a breathless pause, as Mrs. Cratchit, looking at the carving knife, prepared to plunge it into the goose's breast. When she did, and when the long-awaited gush of stuffing spilled out, there was great delight all around the table, and even Tiny Tim, excited by the two young Cratchits, beat on the table with the handle of his knife, and feebly cried "Hurrah!"

Bob said he didn't believe there ever was such a beautiful goose, but the truth was that it was a tiny, pathetic thing, barely a mouthful for each Cratchit. And yet no one complained. They all continued to praise the goose throughout the entire course. Then Miss Belinda changed the plates, and Mrs. Cratchit left to get the pudding.

"Oh, a wonderful pudding!" Bob Cratchit said. Everybody had something kind to say about it, and nobody said it was too small a pudding for such a large family.

At last the dinner was all done. Apples and oranges were put on the table, and as the Cratchit family drew close, Bob proposed: "A Merry Christmas to us all, my dears. God bless us!" which all the family echoed.

"God bless us, everyone!" said Tiny Tim, the last of all.

He sat very close to his father's side on his little stool. Bob held his withered little hand in his, beaming with love for the child, and Bob's face showed that he wished to keep Tim by his side, fearing that he might be taken from him.

"Spirit," said Scrooge, with an interest in his voice that had never been there before, "tell me if Tiny Tim will live."

"I see a vacant seat," replied the Ghost, "and a crutch without an owner, carefully preserved. If these shadows remain unaltered, the child will die."

"No, no," said Scrooge. "Oh, no, kind Spirit! Say he will be spared."

"If these shadows remain unaltered by the future, none other of my race," returned the Ghost, "will find him here."

Scrooge hung his head and was overcome with grief.

"Man," said the Ghost, "if man you are, will you decide what men will live, what men will die? It may be, that in the sight of Heaven, you are more worthless and less fit to live than the millions like this poor man's child!"

Scrooge hung his head at the Ghost's rebuke, and cast his eyes upon the ground. But he raised them again upon hearing his own name.

"Mr. Scrooge!" said Bob. "To Mr. Scrooge, the founder of the feast!"

"The founder of the feast indeed!" cried Mrs. Cratchit, growing red in the cheeks. "I wish I had him here. I'd give him a piece of my mind to feast on, and I hope he'd have a good appetite for it."

"My dear," said Bob, "the children! It's Christmas Day."

"Christmas Day," she said, "is the only day when one would bother drinking the health of such an odious, stingy, hard, unfeeling man as Mr. Scrooge. You know he is, Robert! Nobody knows it better than you do!"

"My dear," was Bob's mild answer, "Christmas Day."

"Very well. I'll drink his health for your sake and the Day's," said Mrs. Cratchit, "not for his. Long life to him! A merry Christmas and a happy new year! He'll be very merry and very happy, I have no doubt!"

The children drank the toast after her, but it appeared no one's heart was truly in it. Tiny Tim drank it last of all, but he didn't care for it. The mention of Scrooge's name cast a dark shadow on the party, which was not dispelled for several minutes.

After it had passed away, they were so much merrier than before, from the mere relief of the toast to Scrooge being over and done with.

They were not a handsome family. They were not well dressed, their shoes were not waterproof, their clothes were scanty, and they very likely knew the inside of a pawnbroker's shop. But, they were happy, grateful, pleased with one another, and contented with the time. When the spotlight on them faded, they looked happier yet, and Scrooge had his eye upon them, and especially on Tiny Tim, until the last.

STEPHEN LOMER

CHAPTER SEVEN

It was a great surprise to Scrooge, in the renewed darkness of the ballroom, to hear a hearty laugh. It was a much greater surprise to Scrooge to recognize it as his own nephew's. As another spotlight lit, Scrooge, with the Spirit standing smiling by his side, saw what appeared to be a bright, dry, conservatory, and looked upon that very nephew!

"Ha ha!" laughed Scrooge's nephew. "Ha ha ha!"

When Scrooge's nephew—for it truly was Scrooge's nephew, who had agreed to take part in the production as readily as the Cratchit family had—laughed this way, holding his sides, rolling his head, and twisting his face into the most extravagant contortions, Scrooge's niece, by marriage, laughed as heartily as he did. And their assembled friends roared out as well.

"Ha ha! I visited his counting house and he said that Christmas was a humbug, I swear it!" cried Scrooge's nephew. "He believed it too!"

"Shame on him, Fred!" said Scrooge's niece, indignantly.

She was very pretty. Exceedingly pretty. She had a dimpled face, a ripe little mouth that seemed made to be kissed, a spray of freckles, and the sunniest pair of eyes you ever saw in any little creature's head.

"He's a funny old fellow," said Scrooge's nephew, "and not particularly pleasant. But his offenses carry their own punishment, and I have nothing to say against him."

"I'm sure he is very rich, Fred," hinted Scrooge's niece. "At least you always tell me so."

"Yes, but so what?" asked Scrooge's nephew. "His wealth is of no use to him. He doesn't do any good with it. He doesn't make himself comfortable with it. He doesn't have the satisfaction of thinking—ha!—that he is ever going to benefit *us* with it."

"I have no patience with him," observed Scrooge's niece. Scrooge's niece's sisters, and all the other ladies, expressed the same opinion.

"Oh, I have!" said Scrooge's nephew. "I am sorry for him. I couldn't be angry with him if I tried. Who suffers by his crotchety nature? He does! He takes it into his head to dislike us, and he won't come and dine with us. What's the consequence? Well, he doesn't lose much of a dinner."

"I think he loses a very good dinner!" interrupted Scrooge's niece. Everybody else said the same, and they must have been competent judges, because they had just had dinner, with the dessert upon a side table.

"As I was saying," said Scrooge's nephew, "the consequence of him disliking us, and not making merry with us, is that he loses some pleasant moments, which could do him no harm. I am sure he loses more pleasant companions than he can find in his own thoughts, or in his moldy old office, or his dusty chambers. I mean to give him the same chance every year, whether he likes it or not, because I pity him. He may curse Christmas until he dies, but if I go to his counting house, in good spirits, year after year, and that inspires him to leave his poor clerk fifty pounds, that's something."

After tea, they had some music, and then after a while they played games. Scrooge's niece sat in a large chair with a footstool, near the edge of the spotlight, and the Ghost and Scrooge were close behind her. She joined in the game of How, When, and Where, and she was very good. There were about twenty people there, young and old, a mix of Fred's actual friends and performers from the company, but they all played the game, and so did Scrooge, who completely forgot that his voice could not be heard. He sometimes shouted out his guesses, and very often guessed right, too. The actors carried on with the performance as though Scrooge were merely a rude, loud-talking guest in the audience at a show.

The Ghost was greatly pleased to find Scrooge in this mood, and Scrooge begged like a boy to be allowed to stay until the guests departed. But the Spirit said this could not be done.

"Oh, they are starting a new game," said Scrooge. "Let us remain one half hour, Spirit, only one!"

It was a game called Yes and No, where Scrooge's nephew had to think of something, and the rest had to guess what, but he could only answer their questions yes or no, as the case was. The questions came very quickly, and revealed that he was thinking of an animal, a live animal, a rather disagreeable animal, a savage animal, an animal that growled and grunted sometimes, and talked sometimes, and lived in London, and walked the streets, and wasn't bred for show, and wasn't led by anybody, and didn't live in a zoo, and was never killed in a market, and was not a horse, or an ass, or a cow, or a bull, or a tiger, or a dog, or a pig, or a cat, or a bear. With every question, his nephew burst into a fresh roar of laughter. At last a guest, one of Fred's sisters-in-law, cried out:

"I have it! I know what it is, Fred! I know what it is!"

"What is it?" cried Fred.

"It's your Uncle Scro-o-o-o-oge!"

Which it certainly was. The guests were pleased with such an enjoyable run, though some objected that the reply to "Is it a bear?" should have been "Yes."

"He has given us plenty of merriment," said Fred, "and it would be ungrateful not to drink to his health. Here is a glass of mulled wine, and I say, Uncle Scrooge!"

"Uncle Scrooge!" they cried.

"A Merry Christmas and a happy New Year to the old man, whatever he is!" said Scrooge's nephew. "He wouldn't take it from me, but he may have it anyway. Uncle Scrooge!"

Scrooge had imperceptibly become so gay and light of heart that he might have thanked the company, if the Ghost had given him time. But the whole scene faded to black in the breath of the last word spoken by his nephew, and he and the Spirit were again alone in the darkness.

Within this dark break, Iain, who you will remember was portraying the Ghost of Christmas Present, left Scrooge's side, and was replaced by a similarly attired but much older and less hearty actor, the effect of which was helped along once again by expert costume and makeup artists. Scrooge looked upon the cragged face, the now-faded robe, and the stooped figure of the Ghost, who leaned heavily on his staff to remain upright.

"Are spirits' lives so short?" asked Scrooge.

"My life upon this globe is very brief," replied the Ghost. "It ends tonight."

"Tonight!" cried Scrooge.

76

"Tonight at midnight. The time is drawing near."

The bell behind the curtain was struck at that moment to create the illusion of three quarters past eleven.

"Forgive me for asking," said Scrooge, looking intently at the Spirit's robe, "but I see something strange, and not belonging to you, protruding from your skirts. Is it a foot or a claw?"

"It might as well be a claw, for all the flesh there is on it," was the Spirit's sorrowful reply. "Look here."

From the folds of his robe, he released two children, who had moments before scurried under the robes from the shadows beyond. They were wretched, abject, frightful, hideous, miserable. If only that could all be attributed to the costumers and the makeup artists, but no—they were true street urchins, brought in to merely act as themselves. They knelt down at the Ghost's feet, and clung to the outside of his garment.

"Look, look, down here!" exclaimed the Ghost.

They were a boy and girl. Yellow, meager, ragged, scowling, and wolfish—where graceful youth should have filled their features out, a stale and shriveled hand, like that of age, had pinched and twisted them, and pulled them into shreds. Where angels might have flown, devils lurked and glared. No perversion of humanity, at any level, through all the mysteries of creation, has had monsters half so horrible and dreadful.

Scrooge stepped back, appalled.

"Spirit! Are they yours?" It seemed Scrooge could say no more.

"They are man's," said the Spirit, looking down upon them. "This boy is Ignorance. This girl is Want. Beware them both, but most of all beware this boy!" cried the Spirit, stretching out his hand. "For on his brow I see written Doom, unless the writing is erased!"

With that proclamation, and Scrooge's wide eyes focused on the Spirit and the terrifying children, a black-clad stagehand behind the old man dosed him once again with a puff of ether. His eyes rolled and he pitched backward, right into waiting arms, who bundled him back off to bed.

CHAPTER EIGHT

"Reset!" cried Edward from his spot behind the curtain, and once again sets and props were moved about with furious speed.

Once everything was arranged, cast and crew were ready and silent as they waited for Scrooge to stir. Just as he did so, however, Belle looked over at the actor who would portray the Ghost of Christmas Yet To Come. He had removed his hood and stood near the ballroom's center window, silently convulsing.

"Your cue!" Edward whispered urgently, not realizing there was an issue, but Belle raced over to the poor man's side.

"What is it?" she asked quietly, for the actor had his fist jammed to his lips and his eyes tightly shut, and his cheeks were puffed out to near comic proportions.

"His lungs," whispered a nearby actress, who bent in to help. "He spent many a year in the mines. 'Tis a coughing fit."

"Your cue!" hissed Edward, coming over to discover the holdup. The man kept coughing silently, without control, and Belle felt a needle of panic pierce her heart. It could not all pull at the seams now, not after all they had done!

"He cannot perform," Belle whispered to Edward. "His lungs have failed him."

"Cannot perform!" Edward whispered back. "No one knows his dialogue well enough besides me!" He was already reaching for the man's costume when Belle grabbed his wrist.

"No!" she whispered urgently. "You are needed here to coordinate!" And without another word, she threw the cloak and hood over herself.

"Belle!" whispered Edward as she made her way to the seam in the curtain. "You know none of his lines!"

She lifted the hood so he could see her smiling face. "Then I will improvise."

Scrooge woke, lifted his eyes, and beheld a solemn Phantom, draped and hooded, coming, like a mist along the ground, toward him. The dark figure was dramatically lit from behind by a spotlight on the floor.

The Phantom slowly, gravely, silently, approached. When it came near him, Scrooge scampered out of bed and bent down on his knee, for the very air through which this Spirit moved seemed heavy with gloom and mystery.

It was shrouded in a deep black garment, which concealed its head, its face, its form, and left nothing of it visible save one outstretched, gloved hand. Aside from this, it would have been difficult to tell the figure from the night, or separate it from the darkness by which it was surrounded.

Its mysterious presence seemed to fill him with a solemn dread, for the Spirit neither spoke nor moved.

Belle was familiar with the ghost's speeches, but would never be able to remember them word-for-word. And even if she could, her fluttery, high-pitched voice would be an immediate giveaway that something was amiss. So she said nothing, merely stood there in her robes, and watched as Scrooge trembled.

Time passed, and Belle began to fret that
they would spend the rest of their days, old
man and spectre, merely staring at one
another in the great ballroom. But then at last,
Scrooge spoke.

"I have thus far been visited by the Ghosts
of Christmas Past and Christmas Present. Are
you the Ghost of Christmas Yet to Come?"

Belle let out a silent sigh of relief, and then
lifted her arm slowly and pointed toward the
darkness with her hand.

"You are about to show me shadows of
the things that have not happened, but will
happen," Scrooge pursued. "Is that right,
Spirit?"

The hood moved almost imperceptibly
down and then back up again, as if the Spirit
had nodded its head. That was the only
answer he received.

Scrooge's legs trembled beneath him, and
he could hardly stand when he prepared to
follow it. The Spirit paused a moment,
observing him, giving him time to recover.

"Ghost of the Future!" he exclaimed, "I
fear you more than any spectre I have seen.
But I know your purpose is to do me good,
and I hope to live to be a different man. I am

prepared to join you, and do it gratefully. Will you not speak to me?"

No, thought Belle. *I most certainly will not.*

The ghost made no reply. Its hand pointed straight ahead.

"Lead on, then!" said Scrooge. "Lead on, Spirit!"

The Phantom moved away as it had come toward him. Scrooge followed in its shadow.

A spotlight lit, illuminating the illusion of a street corner, and The Spirit stopped beside one little group of businessmen. Observing that the hand was pointed to them, Scrooge advanced to listen to them.

"No," said a great fat actor with a monstrous chin, "I don't know much about it, either way. I only know he's dead."

"When did he die?" inquired another.

"Last night, I believe."

"What was the matter with him?" asked a third, taking a vast quantity of snuff out of a very large snuff box. "I thought he'd never die."

"God knows," said the first, with a yawn.

"What has he done with his money?" asked a red-faced gentleman.

"I haven't heard," said the man with the large chin, yawning again. "Left it to his company, perhaps. He hasn't left it to me. That's all I know."

This received a great deal of laughter.

"It's likely to be a very cheap funeral," said the same speaker. "I don't know anybody planning to go to it. Suppose we make up a party and volunteer?"

"I don't mind going if lunch is provided," observed the gentleman with the red face. "But I must be fed if I'm going to attend."

Another laugh.

"Well, I am the least interested among you," said yet another speaker. "I never wear black gloves, and I never eat lunch. But I'll offer to go, if anybody else will. When I come to think of it, I'm not sure that I wasn't his most particular friend, for we used to stop and speak whenever we met. Well, let me know your plans. Farewell!"

Speakers and listeners strolled away, and blended back into the shadows. Scrooge knew the men, and looked toward the Spirit for an explanation.

As this spotlight faded, another, close at hand, blazed. The Phantom glided toward it, its finger pointed to two people meeting. Scrooge listened again, thinking that the explanation might lie here.

84

He knew these men, also, perfectly. They were men of business. Very wealthy, and of great importance. He had always gone out of his way to remain in their good graces—from a business point of view, of course. Strictly from a business point of view.

"How are you?" said one.

"How are you?" returned the other.

"Well!" said the first. "The devil finally got what was coming to him, didn't he?"

"So I am told," returned the second. "Cold, isn't it?"

"Seasonable for Christmastime. Well, I must be off. Good morning!"

"Good morning!"

Not another word. That was their meeting, their conversation, and their parting.

STEPHEN LOMER

CHAPTER NINE

Quiet and dark, beside Scrooge stood the Phantom, with its outstretched hand. They left the busy scene, and went to another pool of light, where Scrooge could see the inside of a pawnbroker's shop. The floor was piled with iron, old rags, bottles, bones, rusty keys, nails, chains, hinges, files, scales, weights, and anything else the set dressers could obtain from the pawnbrokers shops they'd visited in preparation.

Sitting in among all these wares was a tall, thin, ashen-faced man with long gray hair tied back at the shoulders. He had been made up to look nearly seventy, and he smoked a long pipe calmly and thoughtfully.

This man, an actor called Philip, was a great concern to Belle. While Edward had repeatedly assured her that Philip was a consummate professional, Belle had witnessed him in rehearsal acting in a most over-the-top, least believable fashion imaginable. They had created an immersive world that Scrooge had entirely bought into, and Belle feared it could all be undone with one performance.

As Scrooge and the Phantom watched, a woman appeared carrying a heavy bundle. She had hardly set foot inside the circle of light when another woman, also carrying a heavy bundle, arrived, and then a man, dressed in faded black clothes, arrived as well, bearing his own bundle. They looked one to another for a moment or two, and then all three burst out laughing.

"Let the maid go first!" cried the woman who had entered first. "Then the laundress"—here she pointed to herself—"and let the undertaker's assistant go third. What were the odds, old Joe? That we three would meet here without planning it!"

"You couldn't have met in a better place," said Philip as old Joe, removing his pipe from his mouth. "Come into the parlor."

The four of them vanished into the darkness and then reappeared into a new spotlight as the old one dimmed. The parlor set was even shabbier and gloomier than the one that had preceded it.

The first woman threw her bundle on the floor and sat down on a stool, crossing her elbows on her knees, and looking with a bold defiance at the other two.

"Don't you dare feel guilty, Mrs. Dilber!" said the woman. "Every person has a right to take care of themselves. He always did."

"That's true, indeed!" said the laundress. "No man more so."

"Well then, don't stand staring as if you're afraid, woman! Who's the worse for the loss of a few things like these? Not a dead man, surely."

"No, indeed," said Mrs. Dilber, laughing.

"If he wanted to keep them after he was dead, the wicked old screw," pursued the woman, "why wasn't he kinder in his lifetime? If he had been, he'd have had somebody to look after him when he was struck dead, instead of lying there, gasping out his last breath, all alone."

"Truer words were never spoken," said Mrs. Dilber. "It's all he deserves."

"I wish I'd gotten all I deserve," replied the woman. "And I would have, mark my words, if I could have laid my hands on anything else. Open that bundle, old Joe, and let me know what it's worth. Say it aloud, I don't care. We knew that we were helping ourselves, before we met here, I believe. It's no sin. Open the bundle, Joe."

"No," Joe said dramatically, and Belle felt her pulse quicken. She knew there was no moment of Joe refusing to open the maid's bundle.

"Go on, Joe," the actress playing the maid said, flustered, looking to the other actors for help. "Open the bundle."

"No," Joe repeated, now standing and staring off into the darkness as if to launch into a soliloquy. "Many a moon have I known you, my dear, and many a valuable object have you brought into my establishment."

Belle was thankful that the hood covered her face so that Scrooge could not see her roll her eyes. Philip was providing his own dialogue, puffing up his character, to the detriment of the scene.

"Never would I deny myself the anticipation of seeing what you have procured," Philip said, turning back to the scene and addressing the maid, "so let me examine the others' goods before yours."

"Er—all right, then. Have it your way," the maid said.

The man in faded black stepped forward, very clearly annoyed at Philip's improvisation. "Shall I go first then?" he asked, and old Joe nodded. The man opened his small bundle, and Joe took each object out to examine. There were two seals, a pencil case, a pair of sleeve buttons, and a brooch of no great value. Old Joe appraised them all, and then chalked the sums he was willing to pay on a small chalkboard, and totaled them.

"That's your total," said Joe, "and I wouldn't give another sixpence if my life depended upon it." That was the end of his scripted dialogue, but again he embellished. "For I am but a poor pawnbroker, scrabbling about in the muck, hoping only to one day rise above my station and enjoy the life that so many others take for granted."

"*Joe*," said Mrs. Dilber warningly, and whatever else he might have been planning to say died on his tongue under her stare. She held her angry gaze as she offered him her bundle. Sheets and towels, some clothing, two old-fashioned silver teaspoons, a pair of sugar tongs, and some boots. Her account was stated on the chalkboard in the same manner.

"I always give too much to the ladies," old Joe sighed dramatically. "It's a weakness of mine."

"And now undo my bundle, Joe," said the first woman.

Joe knelt down and unfastened a great many knots, dragging out a large and heavy roll of some dark stuff.

"What's this?" said Joe. "Bed curtains?"

"Yes!" returned the woman, laughing and leaning forward on her crossed arms. "Bed curtains!"

"You don't mean to say you took them down, rings and all, with him lying there?" said Joe.

"Yes I do," replied the woman. "Why not?"

"You were born to make a fortune," said Joe, "and you'll certainly do it."

"I certainly won't keep my hands to myself when I can get anything in them by reaching them out. Not for a man like him, I promise you, Joe," returned the woman coolly. "Don't drop that oil on the blankets, now."

"His blankets?" asked Joe.

"Who else's do you think?" replied the woman. "He isn't likely to be cold without them, I dare say."

"I hope he didn't die of anything catching. Eh?" said old Joe, stopping in his work, and looking up.

"Don't you be afraid of that," returned the woman. "I wasn't so fond of his company that I'd hang about long enough to catch something if he did. Ah! You can look through that shirt till your eyes ache but you won't find a hole in it. It's the best he had, and a fine one too. They'd have wasted it, if it hadn't been for me."

"Wasted it?" asked old Joe.

"Putting it on him to be buried in," replied the woman with a laugh. "Somebody was fool enough to do it, but I took it off him."

Scrooge listened to this dialogue in horror. As they sat grouped around their ill-gotten gains in the pool of light from above, he watched them with disgust. He could not have been more revolted by them if they were demons, haggling over the corpse itself.

"Ha!" laughed the same woman as old Joe counted out their money. "You see this? He frightened everyone away from him when he was alive, and we profit now that he's dead! Ha ha ha!"

"Spirit!" said Scrooge, shuddering from head to toe. "I see. I see. The case of this

93

unhappy man might be my own. My life heads that way now. Merciful heaven, what is this?"

He recoiled in terror, for behind him, a softer light than had yet been produced weakly illuminated a bed: a bare, uncurtained bed, on which, beneath a ragged sheet, there lay what could only be a human form.

The pale light fell straight upon the bed, and on it, plundered, unwatched, unwept, uncared for, was the body of this man.

Though the scene was gruesome (for Edward's team had so perfectly formed the figure on the bed that one could scarcely discern it from the real thing), Belle was pleased to see it. It meant they were closing in on the end of the production, and she was growing warm and uncomfortable in her trappings.

Scrooge glanced toward the Phantom, whose hand raised and pointed to the figure's head. The cover was so loose that the slightest movement of it, the motion of Scrooge's finger on it, would have revealed the face. He looked as though he thought about it, but fear kept him rooted to the spot.

"Spirit!" he said. "This is a fearful place. Believe me when I say that the lesson learned here will stay with me. Let us go!"

Still the Ghost pointed with an unmoved finger to the head.

"I understand you," Scrooge returned, "and I would do it, if I could. But I do not have the power, Spirit. I do not have the power."

Again it seemed to look upon him.

"If there is any person in the town who feels emotion caused by this man's death," said Scrooge, "show that person to me, Spirit, please!"

STEPHEN LOMER

CHAPTER TEN

The Phantom spread its dark robe before him for a moment, like a wing, and when it was withdrawn, revealed another staged room, where a mother and her children were.

She was anxiously expecting someone. She walked up and down the room, jumped at every sound, glanced at the clock, and tried in vain to get on with her needlework.

Finally her husband came into the light, a man whose face was careworn and depressed, though he was young. There was a remarkable expression on it now; a kind of serious delight that he struggled to repress.

He sat down at the table, and when she asked him faintly what the news was, he appeared embarrassed how to answer.

"Is it good?" she said, "or bad?"

"Bad," he answered.

"We are ruined?"

"No. There is still hope, Caroline."

"If he relents, there is!" she said, amazed. "There is truly hope if such a miracle has happened."

"He is past relenting," said her husband. "He is dead."

She expressed her gratefulness with a wide smile and clasped hands, though she quietly asked forgiveness for taking pleasure in such a loss. She pressed him for details.

"I went to see him to request a week's extension," he said. "I was met by a half-drunk woman who told me he was very ill, though I assumed that was an excuse to avoid me. But it turns out to have been quite true. He was not only very ill, but dying."

"To whom will our debt be transferred?"

"I don't know. But in the meantime we'll be able to come up with the money, and it's difficult to imagine the next debt-holder will be as grim and miserly as he was. We can sleep with light hearts tonight, Caroline!"

It was a happier house because of this man's death! The only emotion that the Ghost was able to show him, caused by the event, was one of pleasure.

"Let me see some tenderness connected with this death," said Scrooge. "Or that dark chamber we left will be forever etched in my memory."

The Ghost turned, and once again they appeared to be peering directly into poor Bob Cratchit's house, the dwelling they had visited before, though the set designers had aged the walls and the makeup team had aged the mother and the children, who were seated around the table.

It was quiet. Very quiet. The noisy little Cratchits were as still as statues in one corner, and sat looking up at Peter, who was reading. The mother and her daughters were sewing. But they were very quiet.

The mother laid her work on the table, and put her hand up to her face.

"The color black hurts my eyes," said Cratchit's wife. "It makes them weak by candlelight, and I wouldn't let your father see weak eyes when he comes home for the world. It must be nearly time."

"Past it," Peter answered, shutting his book. "But these few last evenings, I think he's walked a little slower than he used to, Mother."

They were very quiet again. At last she said, and in a steady, cheerful voice, that only faltered once:

"He has walked—he had walked with Tiny Tim on his shoulder, very quickly."

"Indeed," cried Peter.

"Indeed," exclaimed another.

"But he was very light to carry," she resumed, focusing on her work, "and his father loved him so much that it was no trouble, no trouble at all. Ah, here is your father at the door!"

Bob, dressed in his shabby overcoat, came in. His wife handed him a cup of tea, and the two young Cratchits climbed up on his knees and laid their small cheeks against his face.

Bob was very cheerful with them, and spoke pleasantly to all the family. He looked at the work on the table, and praised Mrs. Cratchit's speed. "You will be done long before Sunday," he said.

"Sunday! You went today, then, Robert?" said his wife.

"Yes, my dear," returned Bob. "I wish you could have gone. It would have done you good to see how green a place it is. But you'll see it often. I promised him that I would walk there on Sunday. My little child!" cried Bob. "My little child!"

He couldn't help it. He broke down all at once. The family consoled him as best they could, but they also wept bitter tears.

He left the pool of light and another lit nearby, this showing the inside of another room, which was lighted cheerfully, and hung with Christmas decorations. There was a chair set close beside the child, and there were signs of someone having been there recently. Poor Bob sat down in the chair, and when he had thought a little and composed himself, he kissed the little face. He was reconciled to what had happened, and left the tableau, passing from one pool of light to the other and returning to the rest of the family.

They gathered around the table and talked, the girls and Mrs. Cratchit still working. Bob told them of the extraordinary kindness of Mr. Scrooge's nephew, whom he had met only once, and who, meeting him in the street that day, and seeing that he looked a little— "just a little down, you know," said Bob, asked what had happened to distress him. "At which point," said Bob, "because he is one of the kindest men I have ever met, he said 'I am so sorry to hear it, Mr. Cratchit,' he said, 'and terribly sorry for your good wife.' How he ever knew that, I don't know."

"Knew what, my dear?"

"That you were a good wife," replied Bob.

"Everybody knows that!" said Peter.

"Very well observed, my boy!" cried Bob. "I hope they do. 'Terribly sorry,' he said, 'for your good wife. If I can be of service to you in any way,' he said, giving me his card, 'that's where I live. Come see me.' Now, it wasn't," cried Bob, "because of anything he might be able to do for us, but because of his kind demeanor, that this was so delightful. It really seemed as if he had known our Tiny Tim, and felt for us."

"I'm sure he's a good soul!" said Mrs. Cratchit.

"You would be more sure of it, my dear," returned Bob, "if you saw and spoke to him. I wouldn't be at all surprised if he got Peter a better job."

"Hear that, Peter?" said Mrs. Cratchit.

"And then," cried one of the girls, "Peter will meet a lady, and set up a home for himself."

Peter grinned.

"It's just as likely as not," said Bob, "though there's plenty of time for that, my dear. But however and whenever we part from one another, I am sure none of us will forget poor Tiny Tim—the first parting that there was among us."

"Never, Father!" they all cried.

"And I know," said Bob, "I know, my dears, that when we remember how patient and how mild he was, though he was only a little child, we will not quarrel easily among ourselves and forget poor Tiny Tim."

"No, never, Father!" they all cried again.

"I am happy," said Bob, "I am very happy!"

Mrs. Cratchit kissed him, his daughters kissed him, the two young Cratchits kissed him, and he and Peter shook hands.

STEPHEN LOMER

CHAPTER ELEVEN

"Spectre," said Scrooge, "something tells me that our parting moment is at hand. I know it, but I do not know how. Tell me— who was that man we saw lying dead?"

The grandest spotlight now shone upon the largest, the most complicated, and difficult set of them all—a churchyard. The set designers had spent weeks on it. Not only did it need to have the usual trappings, including headstones, bare trees, and earth to walk upon, but it also needed to be easily transported and set up. Edward's team had risen to the challenge magnificently, and as Belle moved toward it, she had to remind herself that it wasn't real.

The Spirit moved slowly and stood among the graves, pointing down to one. Scrooge

105

advanced toward it, trembling. The Phantom was exactly as it had been, but he feared that he saw new meaning in its solemn shape.

"Before I approach that stone to which you point," said Scrooge, "answer me one question. Are these the shadows of the things that *will* be, or are they shadows of things that *may* be?"

Still the Ghost pointed downward to the grave by which it stood.

"A man's life will follow a certain course," said Scrooge. "But if he departs from that course, the outcome will change. Say it is so with what you show me!"

The Spirit was immovable as ever.

Scrooge crept toward it, trembling as he went, and following the finger, read upon the stone of the neglected grave his own name: Ebenezer Scrooge.

"Am I that man who lay upon the bed?" he cried, falling to his knees.

The finger pointed from the grave to him, and back again.

"No, Spirit! Oh no!"

The finger was still there.

"Spirit!" he cried, falling at the hem of its robes, "hear me! I am not the man I was. I will not be the man I would have been

106

without this intervention. Why show me this if I am past all hope?"

For the first time the hand appeared to shake. It fit the moment, but in truth, Belle was sweating and breathless under the robes, and could not hold her hand steady.

"Good Spirit," Scrooge pursued, "assure me that I can change these shadows you have shown me through an altered life!"

Belle's hand continued to tremble.

"I will honor Christmas in my heart, and try to keep it all year long. I will honor the Past, the Present, and the Future. The Spirits of all three will live in me. I will not ignore the lessons they've taught. Oh, tell me I may remove the writing on this stone!"

Holding up his hands in a last prayer to have his fate reversed, Belle took advantage of his tightly closed eyes and sprayed from within the robe's folds the strongest dose of ether yet. Scrooge fell to the ground among the false headstones, thoroughly unconscious. He lay there for but a moment before four strong pairs of hands hoisted him and bustled him off toward the grand staircase, intent on returning him at long last to his own bed. Belle yanked off the robes and the hood and enjoyed great, gulping whoops of cool air.

107

"Break down!" Edward called out, and a dizzying ballet of movement was under way. Furniture that was borrowed from elsewhere in Scrooge's house was returned from whence it came; the spotlights and the black curtains covering the windows were lowered and repackaged; trunks filled with props, makeup, and costumes were stored and secured; the set pieces were broken down and lashed. Every available hand pitched in, even the Cratchit family, Fred and his wife and friends, Mister Dickens, and the tiniest actors who had portrayed Little Fan and Tiny Tim ran here and there, loading up all they could for transport.

Edward and Belle made one last inspection of the ballroom before nodding and announcing that they would all be heading back to the theatre. As one, laden with as much as any group could possibly be tasked to carry, they made their way as silently through the lobby as they had upon their arrival. With Edward and Belle at the head of the column, they poured out of Scrooge's front door and out into the snowy, darkened street.

And directly into a constable, walking his beat.

"'Ere," the constable said, as the entire company came up short. "'Ere, now, woss goin' on?"

"Oh!" cried Belle. "Constable—?"

"Codswalley."

"Of course, Constable Codswalley. A, er, Merry Christmas to you!"

"Never min' 'at," the constable said. "Whot are you lot up to?"

He squinted in the darkness and saw the troupe with innumerable objects in their arms, all staring rather guiltily. The constable's eyes widened and he reached into his pocket to withdraw his whistle.

"You lot!" he cried. "Don' you move!"

As he raised the whistle to his lips, Belle caught the man's elbow and stopped him, firmly but gently.

"Constable Codswalley," she said patiently. "I realize how this must appear. But I assure you, we are breaking no laws nor committing any crimes. I implore you—accompany us to the theatre, only a short way from here, and I promise I will explain everything in the utmost detail. None of us will attempt to flee."

Constable Codswalley eyed her beadily, but did not attempt to raise his whistle any higher.

"We will be partaking of my wife's delicious hot toddies," Edward chimed in. "You would be more than welcome to join us."

"You do look cold," Belle added.

The constable teetered on the edge of indecision, but apparently desiring a hot drink and an explanation more than the hassle of rounding up more than a hundred souls on Christmas Eve, he replaced his whistle in his pocket and leveled a finger at Belle.

"Righ'," he said. "But this story be'er be good."

Several hours later, in the warm glow of the theatre's lights, raucous laughter and joyful conversation echoed off the walls as the members of the troupe and non-members alike toasted to each other's good health and recounted the thrills of the night's adventure.

Constable Codswalley, who had found the honest explanation of the night's events highly amusing, lay passed out in the orchestra pit, several of Edward's wife's toddies flowing through his bloodstream.

Belle had assumed that once the group had successfully returned to the theatre and all of the accoutrements had been stored away, they would enjoy a quick toast and then each would return to his or her own home to celebrate what remained of Christmas Eve. But no! They all seemed loathe to leave, so the celebration continued well into Christmas morning.

Chatting gaily with the Ghost of Christmas Past and both Ghosts of Christmas Present, who all looked quite ordinary now, Belle was surprised to hear the church bell toll six.

"Goodness!" she cried, hastening up the aisle toward the front doors. "He'll likely be awake any moment. I must see for myself if we accomplished our goal. Wish me good fortune!"

CHAPTER TWELVE

All the souls in the theatre did wish her good fortune as she ventured out into the cold of Christmas morning. She made her way carefully but resolutely down the cobblestones until she reached the corner of Scrooge's house, just below his bedroom window but out of sight.

She stood there no more than a minute when she heard a commotion coming from above. Her heart quickened. Had her plan worked?

"Oh Jacob Marley! Heaven and Christmastime be praised!" she heard Scrooge cry, and her hand went to her lips where, unbidden, a wide smile had blossomed. "I say it on my knees, old Jacob, on my knees!"

Belle laughed to herself, for she knew how loudly he must be shouting for her to hear him through closed second-story windows.

"They are not torn down," cried Scrooge, and Belle could see him in her mind's eye, admiring the intact bed curtains. "They are not torn down, rings and all. They are here—I am here—the shadows of the things that would have been may be dispelled. They will be. I know they will!"

She could scarcely believe she was hearing the same man, and her heart was so glad of it.

"I don't know what to do!" cried Scrooge, laughing and crying in the same breath. "I am as light as a feather! I am as happy as an angel! I am as merry as a schoolboy! I am as giddy as a drunken man! A merry Christmas to everybody! A happy New Year to all the world. Whoop! Ha ha ha!"

For a man who had been out of practice for so many years, it was a splendid laugh, a most boisterous laugh!

"I don't know what day of the month it is!" said Scrooge. "I don't know how long I've been among the Spirits. I don't know anything. I'm quite a baby. Never mind! I don't care! I'd rather be a baby! Whoop!"

Suddenly, the window above her flew open, clearing away the accumulated snow on the sill so that it landed squarely on Belle's head, and Scrooge appeared.

"What's today!" cried Scrooge, calling down to a boy in his Sunday clothes, walking alone along the street.

"Eh?" returned the boy, confused.

"What's today, my fine fellow?" said Scrooge.

"Today?" replied the boy. "Why, Christmas Day."

"It's Christmas Day!" said Scrooge. "I haven't missed it. The Spirits have done it all in one night. They can do anything they like. Of course they can. Of course they can. Hello, my fine fellow!"

"Hello!" returned the boy.

"Do you know the poultry shop, the next street over, on the corner?" Scrooge inquired.

"I should hope so," replied the lad.

"An intelligent boy!" said Scrooge. "A remarkable boy! Do you know whether they've sold the prize turkey that was hanging up there? Not the little prize turkey. The big one?"

"What, the one as big as me?" returned the boy.

115

STEPHEN LOMER

"What a delightful boy!" said Scrooge.
"It's a pleasure to talk to you. Yes, my lad!"
"It's hanging there now," replied the boy.
"Is it?" said Scrooge. "Go and buy it."
"You're barking!" exclaimed the boy.
"No, no," said Scrooge, "I mean it. Go
and buy it, and tell them to bring it here so I
can give them directions where to take it.
Come back with the man, and I'll give you a
shilling. Come back with him in less than five
minutes and I'll give you half a crown!"

The boy was off like a shot. Belle's heart
swelled at the sight of him.

"I'll send it to Bob Cratchit's!" said
Scrooge, rubbing his hands with a laugh. "He
won't know who sent it. It's twice the size of
Tiny Tim. What a laugh sending it to Bob's
will be!"

Belle was so lost in joyful reverie that she
was nearly discovered when Scrooge came
downstairs to open the street door, ready for
the coming of the poultry man. She hid
herself around the corner and watched from
afar as he stood there, awaiting the man's
arrival, examining the knocker on the door
with a grin.

"I will love it, as long as I live!" cried
Scrooge, patting it with his hand. "I hardly

116

ever looked at it before. What an honest expression it has in its face! It's a wonderful knocker! Here's the turkey! Hello! Whoop! How are you? Merry Christmas!"

What a turkey! He never could have stood upon his legs, that bird. He would have snapped them off in a minute, like matches.

"Why, it's impossible to carry that to Camden Town," said Scrooge. "You must have a cab."

The chuckle with which he said this, and the chuckle with which he paid for the turkey, and the chuckle with which he paid for the cab, and the chuckle with which he paid the boy, were only exceeded by the chuckle with which he closed the door and hurried off upstairs. Belle, filled to the brim with joy, took her leave and made her way as quickly as she could back to the theatre. She found herself surrounded by wide eyes and bated breath, and when she smiled and nodded vigorously, there was an explosion of happiness from every soul gathered there.

Belle and her family returned home, tired but happy, and went about preparing for their Christmas dinner. They expected company, but not nearly as much as they got. Members of the troupe kept popping in to relate stories and sightings of Mr. Scrooge.

One young fellow told her that Scrooge had dressed "all in his best" and had at last gotten out into the streets. Scrooge regarded everyone he passed with a delighted smile. He looked so irresistibly pleasant, so the young fellow related, that three or four good-humored gentlemen said, "Good morning, sir! A merry Christmas to you!" and Scrooge said the words right back to them.

A young girl told the story to Belle of Scrooge encountering one of the portly gentlemen he had turned away from his counting house the day before, the gentlemen whose only purpose had been to collect for the poor and destitute.

"My dear sir," the young girl quoted Scrooge, "how do you do? I hope you succeeded yesterday. It was very kind of you. A merry Christmas to you, sir!"

"Mr. Scrooge?" the man had asked, bewildered.

"Yes," said Scrooge. "That is my name, and I fear it may not be pleasant to you. Beg my pardon. And will you have the goodness"—here Scrooge whispered in his ear.

"Lord bless me!" cried the gentleman, as if his breath were taken away. "My dear Mr. Scrooge, are you serious?"

"I am," said Scrooge. "Not a farthing less. A great many back payments are included in it, I assure you. Will you do me that favor?"

"My dear sir," said the other, shaking hands with him. "I don't know what to say to such generosity!"

"Don't say anything, please," retorted Scrooge. "Come and see me. Will you come and see me?"

"I will!" cried the old gentleman. And it was clear he meant to do it.

"Thank you," said Scrooge. "I am much obliged to you. I thank you fifty times. Bless you!"

Belle could hardly believe the stories of the change in Scrooge, and found herself watching the door, hoping for the next sighting of the old man's extraordinary transformation.

According to the next few reports, Scrooge went to church, and walked along the streets, and watched the people hurrying to and fro, and patted children on the head, and greeted beggars, and looked down into the kitchens of houses, and up to the windows, and seemed to find that everything made him happy.

CHAPTER THIRTEEN

That afternoon, Belle made a quick trip to Fred's house to share the latest news about his uncle Scrooge. But Belle had barely removed her cloak when a knock came at the door. The moment she heard Scrooge's voice, she stepped back and blended into the shadows where she could not be seen.

"Is your master at home, my dear?" said Scrooge to the girl who had moments before ushered Belle in.

"Yes, sir."

"Where is he, my love?" said Scrooge.

"He's in the dining room, sir, along with mistress. I'll show you upstairs, if you please."

"Thank you. He knows me," said Scrooge, with his hand already on the dining room doorknob. "I'll go in here, my dear."

He turned it gently, and peeked his face in, around the door.

"Fred!" said Scrooge.

"Why bless my soul!" cried Fred. "Who's that?"

"It's me. Your uncle Scrooge. I have come to dinner. Will you let me in, Fred?"

Let him in! It is a mercy Fred didn't shake his arm off. He was at home immediately. Nothing could have been heartier. His niece looked just the same. So did everyone when they came. A wonderful party filled with wonderful happiness! Belle, observing that Fred could now see for himself the change in Scrooge, quietly let herself out.

That evening, Belle's home was filled to capacity with guests. Edward and his wife and family were there; Charles Dickens and his brood; the Cratchits; friends and family unbound. Belle wanted a private word with Dickens, but in the crowded merriment she was not afforded the opportunity, and so invited him to dinner the following night.

"So, Charles," Belle said as they helped themselves to pudding, "your brilliant writing produced a triumphant production. You must be so proud."

Dickens nodded. "Indeed I am. I only hope that the change in Scrooge is lasting, and that all may benefit by it."

"Mister Dickens?" asked Mary, Belle's daughter. "The night at Mister Scrooge's house, I saw you listening earnestly to what Mister Scrooge said and writing in a fever as the production progressed. Why?"

Dickens smiled. "I was recording Scrooge's words. I had thought to perhaps add them to the existing story and publish the entire adventure as a book."

"Oh dear!" Belle cried, laughing. "Please refrain until after Ebenezer has shuffled off this mortal coil! If he ever knew!"

The whole table laughed at this, and was only interrupted by an urgent knocking at the front door. Belle answered it, and to her surprise, welcomed in an agitated Bob Cratchit. Leading him to the table to join them, Belle asked what was troubling him.

"Mister Scrooge was early to the counting house this morning," Bob conveyed, "and I was late. A full eighteen minutes past the hour ..."

Belle pictured the scene in her head as Bob described it.

"Cratchit!" growled Scrooge, in his accustomed voice. "What do you mean by coming here at this time of day?"

"I am very sorry, sir," said Bob. "I am behind my time."

"You are," said Scrooge. "Yes. I think you are. Step this way, sir, if you please."

"It's only once a year, sir," pleaded Bob. "It will not be repeated. I was making rather merry yesterday, sir."

"Now I'll tell you what, my friend," said Scrooge, "I am not going to stand for this sort of thing any longer. And therefore," he continued, leaping from his stool, and giving Bob such a poke in the chest that he staggered backward. "And therefore ... I am about ... to *raise your salary!*"

Bob trembled, for he had convinced himself that Scrooge had reverted back to the Scrooge of old. Upon the old man's last words, Bob's chest unclenched and he breathed a deep sigh of relief.

"A merry Christmas, Bob!" said Scrooge, with an earnestness that could not be mistaken, as he clapped him on the back. "A merrier Christmas, Bob, my good fellow, than I have given you in many years! I'll raise your salary, and assist your struggling family, and we will discuss your affairs this very afternoon, over a Christmas bowl of Smoking Bishop, Bob! Light the fires, and buy another coal-scuttle before you dot another *i*, Bob Cratchit!"

"Well that's wonderful!" Belle cried at the end of Bob's story. "Isn't it?"

"Mister Scrooge, more than anything else, wishes to help Tiny Tim become well again."

A silence descended upon the table. Belle looked at Dickens who looked at Bob.

"Oh dear," Dickens said softly. "An unforeseen complication."

"We cannot have him suspect," Belle said, more to herself than anyone. "We must think of something."

They all sat in silent contemplation for a short while, and then Dickens said to Bob, "The Tiny Tim character I created was based on a poor crippled orphan I observed when I toured the London Orphanage. If Scrooge is sincere in raising your salary and providing aid to your family, what would you say to bringing that poor lad into the Cratchit household?"

Bob's face lit up.

"Why ... that would be extraordinary!" he exclaimed. "We surely have enough love among us for one more!"

"I don't know the young man's name," Dickens said, "and perhaps he has none to speak of, but either way, he would surely be willing to be known as Tiny Tim if it meant he could have a proper family."

Bob's face was joyful. "Will you see to the details, Mister Dickens? Will you?"

"Of course, Bob. I am only too happy to have one less orphan in this wicked old world."

And so the Cratchits welcomed the young man—who, by the purest and most serendipitous of circumstances, was called Tim—into their hearth and home. And to him, Mister Scrooge became like a second father. He did not die. He lived a long and happy life with the Cratchit family, who never thought of him as anything but one of their own.

Belle kept the truth of the matter to herself for the rest of her days, as did Edward and everyone else involved in the production, though they did talk of it and laugh about it amongst themselves.

Scrooge became as good a friend, as good a master, and as good a man, as the good old city knew, or any other good old city, town, or borough, in the good old world.

Until the end of his days, it was always said of Scrooge that he knew how to keep Christmas well, more than any man alive. May that be truly said of all of us!

And so, as Tiny Tim observed—God bless us, everyone!

ALSO AVAILABLE
BY STEPHEN LOMER

Stargazer Lilies or Nothing at All

Typo Squad

Typo Squad Book II:
Return of the Wordmonger

Typo Squad Book III:
The Typo Alliance

Hell's Nerds and Other Tales

POST A REVIEW!

The best way you can show your support
for an author—besides buying and enjoying
his or her books, of course—is to post a
review on Amazon.

If you enjoyed *Belle's Christmas Carol*, please
post a review today. Thank you!

ABOUT THE AUTHOR

A grammar nerd, *Star Trek* fan, and other things that chicks dig, Stephen Lomer is the author of the hugely popular *Typo Squad* series, the short story collections *Stargazer Lilies or Nothing at All* and *Hell's Nerds and Other Tales*, and the holiday novella *Belle's Christmas Carol*. He also has featured stories in the anthologies *UnCommon Evil*, *Once Upon a Time in Gravity City*, and *Dystopian States of AMERICA*.

Stephen is the creator, owner, and a regular contributor to the website Television Woodshed, and host of the YouTube series Tell Me About Your Damn Book. He's a hardcore fan of the Houston Texans, despite living in the Hub of the Universe his whole life, and believes Mark Twain was correct about pretty much everything.

Stephen lives on Boston's North Shore with his wife, Teresa.

Made in the USA
Monee, IL
10 December 2022

20633821R00079